TRUNDLEBERRY

MR BOUNCER'S
HOUSE

FIRE
STATION

BLODGER'S
GATEHOUSE

SIGMUND SWAMP'S
HOUSE & BOATHOUSE

FERNYBANK FERRY

BROCK GRUFFY'S
SHOP

BRAMBLE'S FARM

CHURCH

VICARAGE

RAILWAY STATION

P.C. HOPPIT'S
HOUSE

POLICE
STATION

DR. BUSHY'S
HOUSE

N
W E
S

This book belongs to:

....

THE FLOATING RESTAURANT

Written & Illustrated by John Patience

PUBLISHED BY PETER HADDOCK LIMITED, BRIDLINGTON, ENGLAND.
© FERN HOLLOW PRODUCTIONS LIMITED
PRINTED IN BELGIUM
ISBN 0-7105-0681-3

One morning Brock Gruffy received a letter from his cousin, Bill. It read:

Dear Brock,
As you know, I am very fond of sailing. Recently I have acquired a new boat and I thought you might like my old one. You'll find it on the river, by the old jetty.
Happy sailing!
Yours, Bill.

When Brock saw the boat he was rather disappointed. It was badly in need of repair. But the badger was struck with a wonderful idea. "I'll turn it into a floating restaurant," he thought.

So, with the help of his old friend Sigmund Swamp, who was very keen to be the waiter on the floating restaurant, Brock set to work.

"It's perfect," said Sigmund when the repairs were finished. "All we need now are customers!"

8

Sigmund drew up some posters to advertise the restaurant and Brock went round the village pasting them up. That evening the first customers arrived. They were the Bouncers and the Willowbanks, having a meal out to celebrate Mr Willowbank's birthday. Sigmund took the orders and, while Brock was busy with the cooking, he played his piano accordion and sang. It was not a great success, but Sigmund didn't appear to notice this.

Brock soon had the cooking done. Sigmund served the meal and everyone was delighted. "Delicious!" exclaimed Mrs Bouncer. "I do love carrot stew, don't you?"

Later, Sigmund appeared with a beautiful birthday cake which Brock had cooked in advance for Mr Willowbank. By this time a wind had sprung up and the water was getting a bit choppy. The barge was rolling a little and, as he came across the deck, Sigmund lost his balance. His feet shot from under him and the cake flew up into the air and came down on top of Mr Willowbank's head!

"Whoops!" said Sigmund. "Happy Birthday."

The customers left the restaurant in a very bad
mood indeed. "Well, that's that," said Brock.
"No-one's going to want to eat here again." It
was getting late so Brock and Sigmund decided to
call it a day. They climbed into their bunks and
fell fast asleep.

In the night the wind grew steadily stronger. It
began to rain. The thunder rolled and the
lightning flashed. Then CRASH, an old tree was
struck and fell into the river. The fallen tree
dammed up the river and the water began to rise.
At last the River Ferny burst its banks and
poured down into Fern Hollow, carrying the
restaurant and the sleeping friends with it!

Sigmund and Brock awoke next morning to the sound of frenzied hooting and cries for help. Imagine their surprise when they went up on deck and found themselves floating through Fern Hollow, just outside Boris Blinks's book shop! The village was flooded.

Boris and Leapy Lizard had taken refuge up on their rooftop. Precarious piles of valuable books which they had managed to save were balanced all around them. "Hoot, hoot! Save us, save us!" cried Boris, flapping his wings hysterically.

Sigmund and Brock lost no time in beginning the rescue operation. After Boris and Leapy there were many other animals to help. Everyone in the village had been forced to take refuge up in their bedrooms or on their rooftops. Sigmund and Brock took them on board and ferried them to the safety of higher ground.

Later, the two heroes discovered the fallen tree damming up the river. "That's the cause of the flood," said Sigmund. "I think we are going to need the help of Farmer Bramble to move it."

Bramble Farm was on high ground and had not been affected by the flood. The farmer soon arrived on his tractor. He attached a strong chain to the tree and pulled it out of the river.

Now the Ferny was flowing freely again. The floodwater would go down, but that would take some time. Meanwhile the Fern Hollow animals were all sitting around, feeling miserable.

"I know how to cheer everyone up," said Brock,
and he disappeared down into the galley. A little
while later the air was filled with the delicious
smell of his cooking. Brock had made a
marvellous vegetable casserole – enough to feed
the whole village. Suddenly everyone was happy
again. There would be lots of work to do,
cleaning up Fern Hollow when the floodwater
had gone down, but in the meantime they were
all having fun at the floating restaurant.

Fern Hollow

MR CHIPS'S HOUSE

MR WILLOWBANK'S
COBBLER'S SHOP

MR CROAKER'S WATERMILL

STRIPEY'S HOUSE

SCHOOL

RIVER FERNY

THE JOLLY VOLE
HOTEL

MR ACORN'S
BAKERY

MR RUSTY'S HOUSE

MR PRICKLES'S HOUSE

POST OFFICE

BORIS BLINKS'S
BOOKSHOP

MR TWINKLE'S
HOUSE

MR TUTTLEBEE'S
SHOP

MR THIMBLE'S
TAILORS SHOP

WINDYWOOD